THE ADVENTURES OF
PLONK

by

JOAN M. DAVIES MFPS

Copyright © 2016 Elizabeth Gordon

The moral right of the author has been asserted.

Apart from any fair dealing for the purposes of research or private study, or criticism or review, as permitted under the Copyright, Designs and Patents Act 1988, this publication may only be reproduced, stored or transmitted, in any form or by any means, with the prior permission in writing of the publishers, or in the case of reprographic reproduction in accordance with the terms of licences issued by the Copyright Licensing Agency. Enquiries concerning reproduction outside those terms should be sent to the publishers.

This is a work of fiction. Names, characters, businesses, places, events and incidents are either the products of the author's imagination or used in a fictitious manner. Any resemblance to actual persons, living or dead, or actual events is purely coincidental.

Matador
9 Priory Business Park,
Wistow Road, Kibworth Beauchamp,
Leicestershire. LE8 0RX
Tel: 0116 279 2299
Email: books@troubador.co.uk
Web: www.troubador.co.uk/matador
Twitter: @matadorbooks

ISBN 978 1785898 921

British Library Cataloguing in Publication Data.
A catalogue record for this book is available from the British Library.

Printed by Cambrian Print, Llandudno, Wales
Typeset in Garamond by Troubador Publishing Ltd, Leicester, UK

Matador is an imprint of Troubador Publishing Ltd

I, Elizabeth Gordon the copyright holder, dedicate the republishing of "The Adventures of Plonk" to my dear late Mother Joan M. Davies MFPS the author and illustrator of this treasured little book

Once upon a time there was a Plonk… Where he came from, nobody knew, and why he was called Plonk nobody could tell.

He lived all by himself on a lonely island in the middle of the sea, and in Summertime his one delight was to bathe in the lovely clear cool water.

And in Wintertime he loved to skate over the ice and play about in the thick snow.

Many ships passed by, but none of them called to see him.

This made Plonk very sad and lonely so he sat down and cried and cried… but at that moment, a witch was flying just above his head on a broom stick,

and before Plonk knew where he was, he was being carried high up into the sky… The witch never spoke, and Plonk was very frightened because he had no idea where he was going.

He was taken to the witch's castle, which was right at the top of a huge rock, which was connected by a thin wooden ladder to the outside world, where boys and girls and grown up people lived.

But Plonk became so miserable. The witch made him run all her errands, and the shopping-basket was always so full of parcels that it was much too heavy for him to carry.

One day, Plonk was on his way home from the market with a basketful of fruit, when he suddenly felt very hungry; and when nobody was looking, he stopped and began to eat one of the oranges.

He enjoyed it so much that he took another, and another, until by and by not a single bit of fruit was left in the basket. But soon Plonk felt more unhappy than ever, because he knew it was wicked to steal.

And so, being too frightened to return home to the witch, he ran away… on and on he went, faster and faster…

… until he was stopped by a pony-man who tied a rope around his neck and led him down the cliffs to the sands.

Poor Plonk, very hot and tired, had to stand side by side with the ponies. He had to work very hard too…

… but he was such a great favourite with the children, that the ponies were very jealous and so they would have nothing to do with him. So once more Plonk was very unhappy and again he ran away.

At last he was caught by a farmer, who, being in need of a horse to pull his hay cart, thought that Plonk would do just as well, and so he had to work even harder than before.

So once more Plonk was very sorry for himself, and again he ran away. This time he met a little gnome who asked for a ride to the end of the lane. "Certainly," said Plonk, "and I am ever so unhappy".

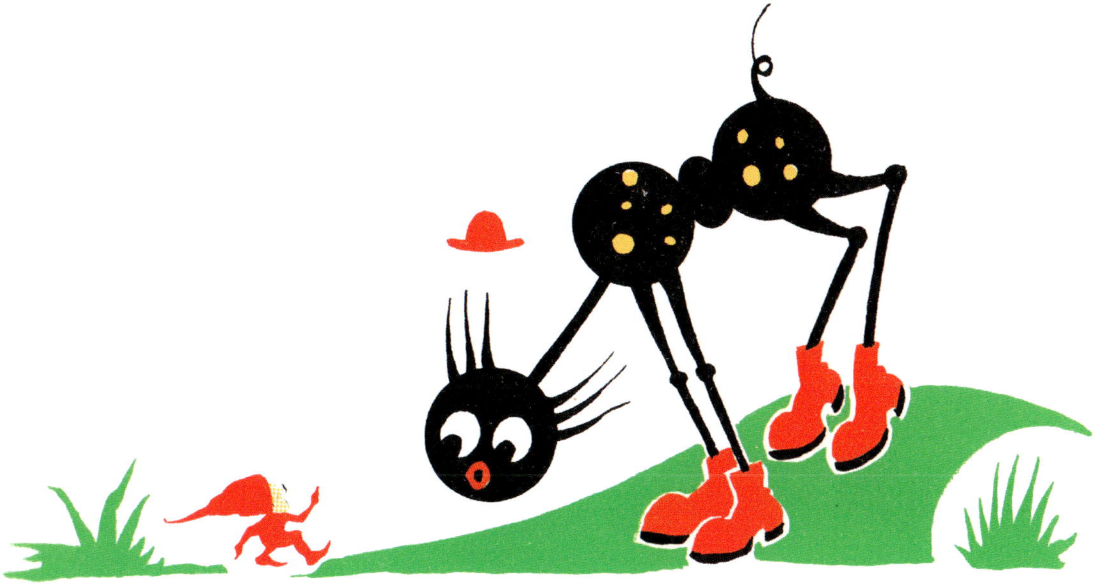

"Could you show me how to get back to my island in the middle of the sea?" said Plonk.

"One good turn deserves another," the gnome replied, and he climbed up Plonk's front leg on to his back.

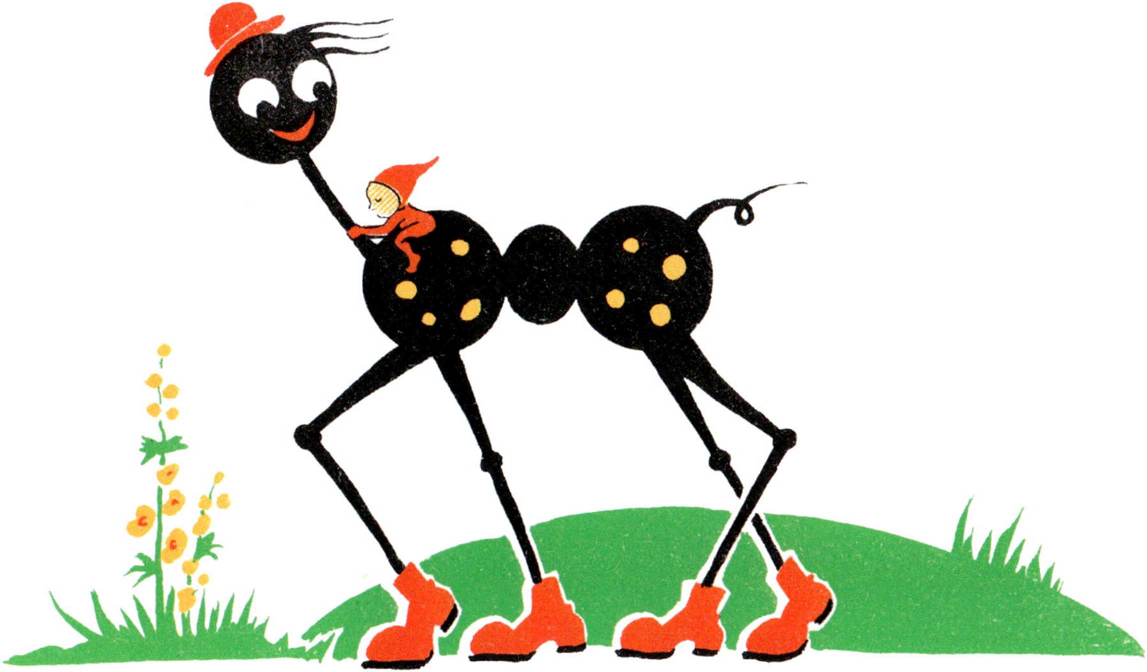

And when they reached the end of the lane, the gnome climbed down. "Thank you very much," he said. "Now if you run down to the jetty I will ask my friend the Good Fairy to help you get home."

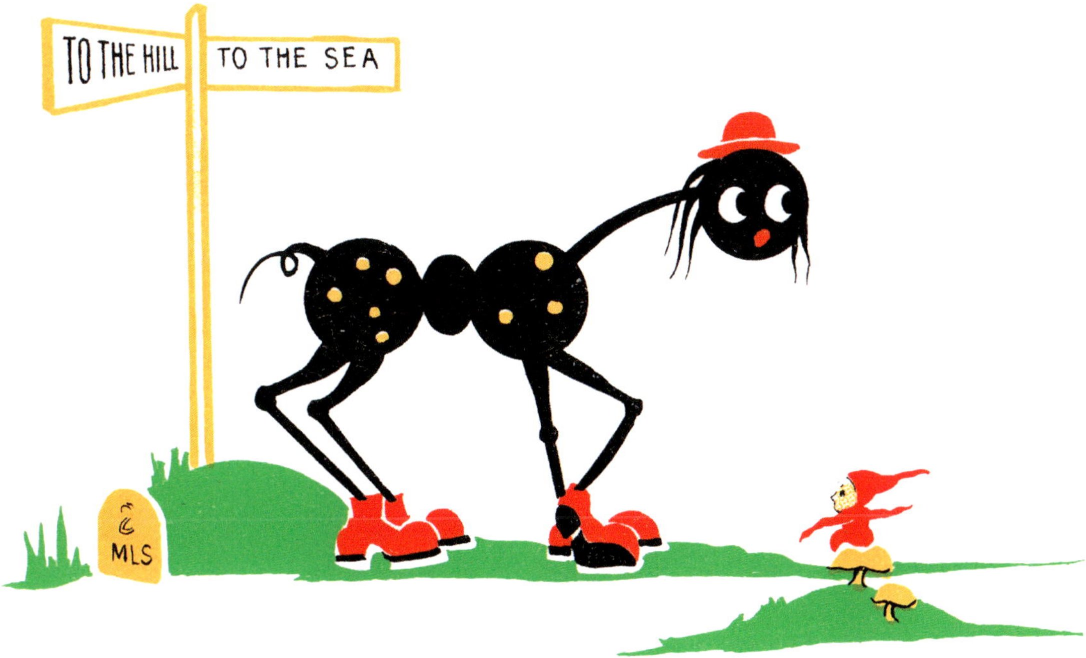
TO THE HILL
TO THE SEA
MLS

Plonk thanked him and did as he said. Just then the Good Fairy arrived.

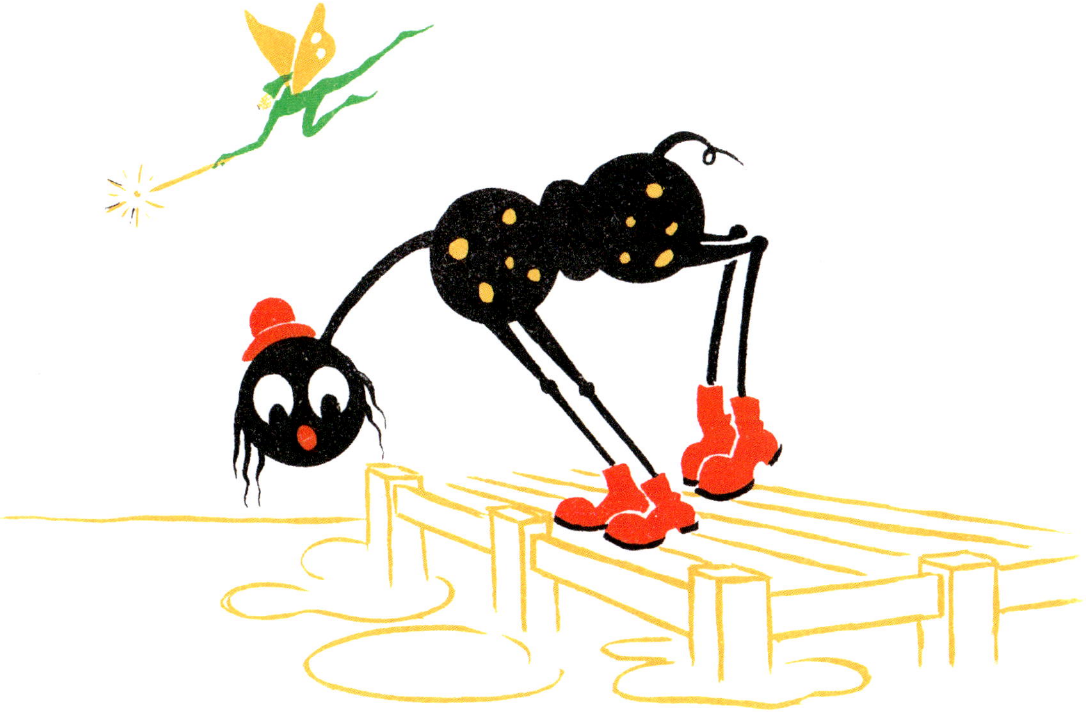

"Now Plonk," she said, "You must first of all, promise me never to steal again…"

"I promise," he cried, and the fairy then led him to a magic boat. Plonk was so excited he just danced for joy.

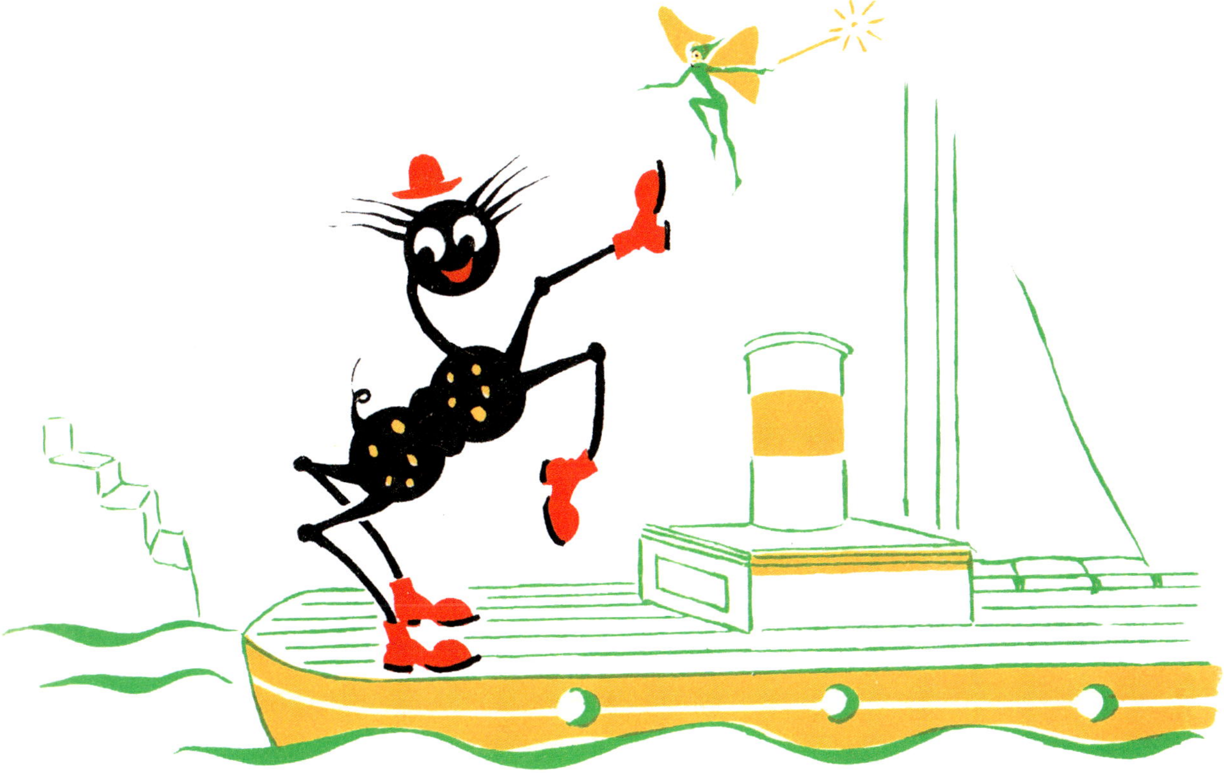

Then the fairy waved her wand, and the boat started to sail...

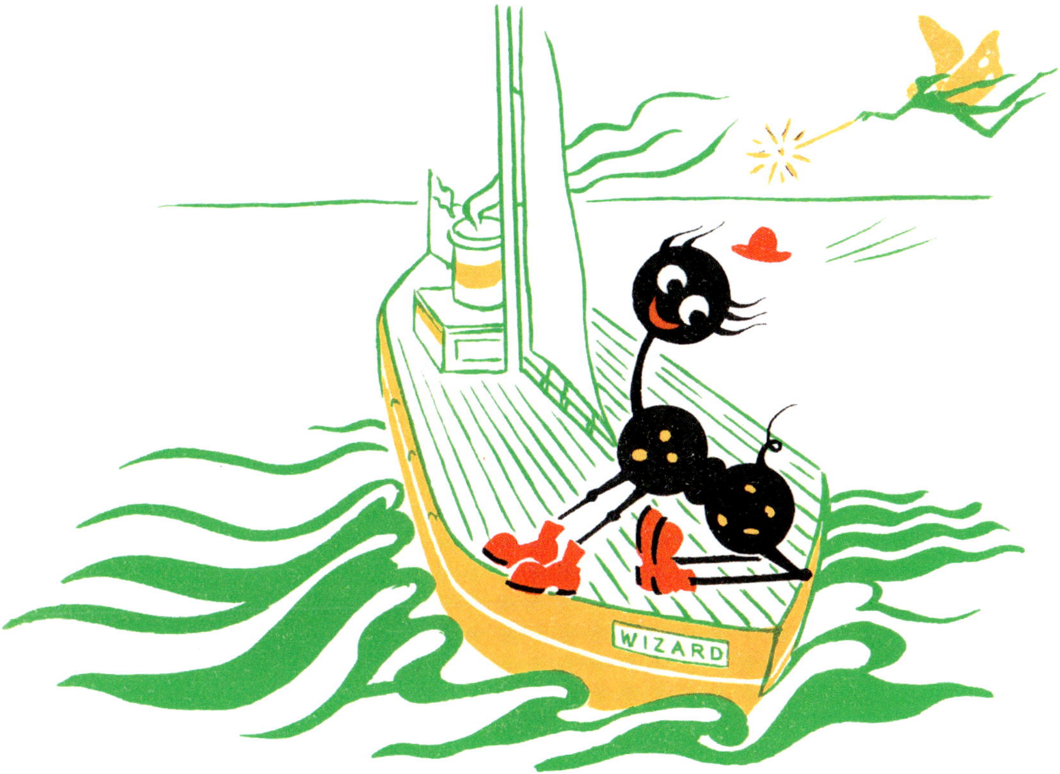
WIZARD

... and so Plonk set foot on his island once again. He was happy at last... at least, he thought he was, until...

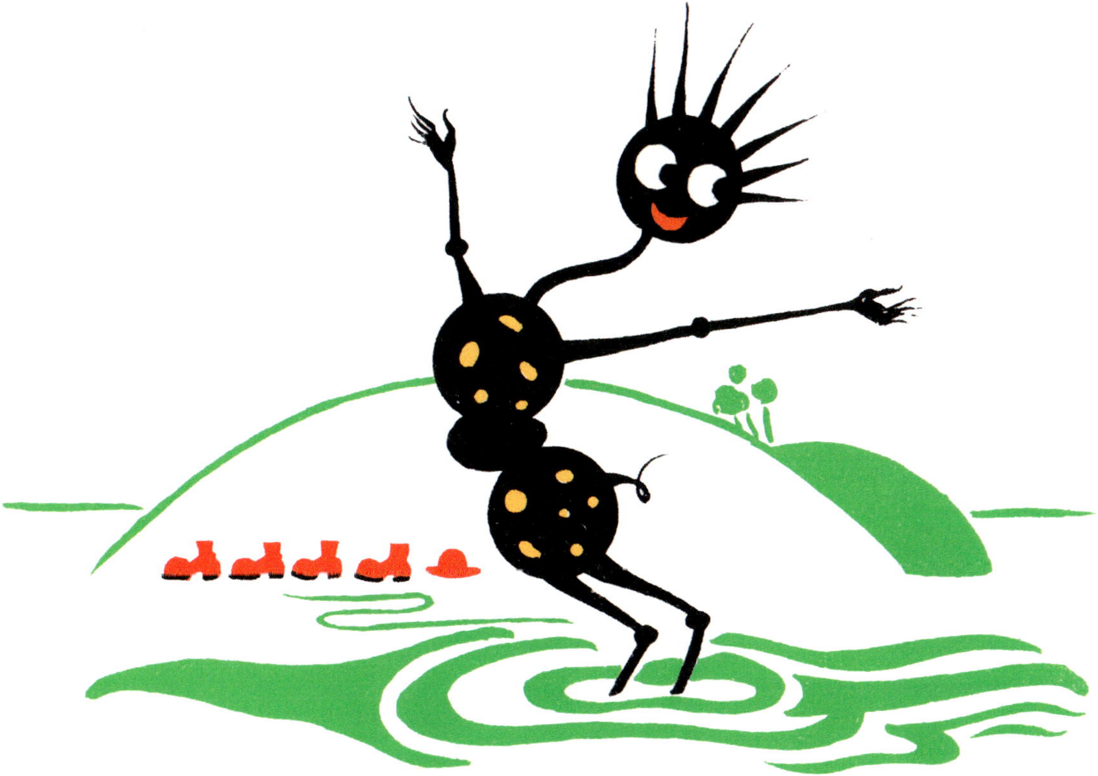

One day while he sat fishing, he once again began to feel very lonely, but luckily for Plonk the Good Fairy was still flying near about and knowing how lonely he felt, she thought of a grand idea.

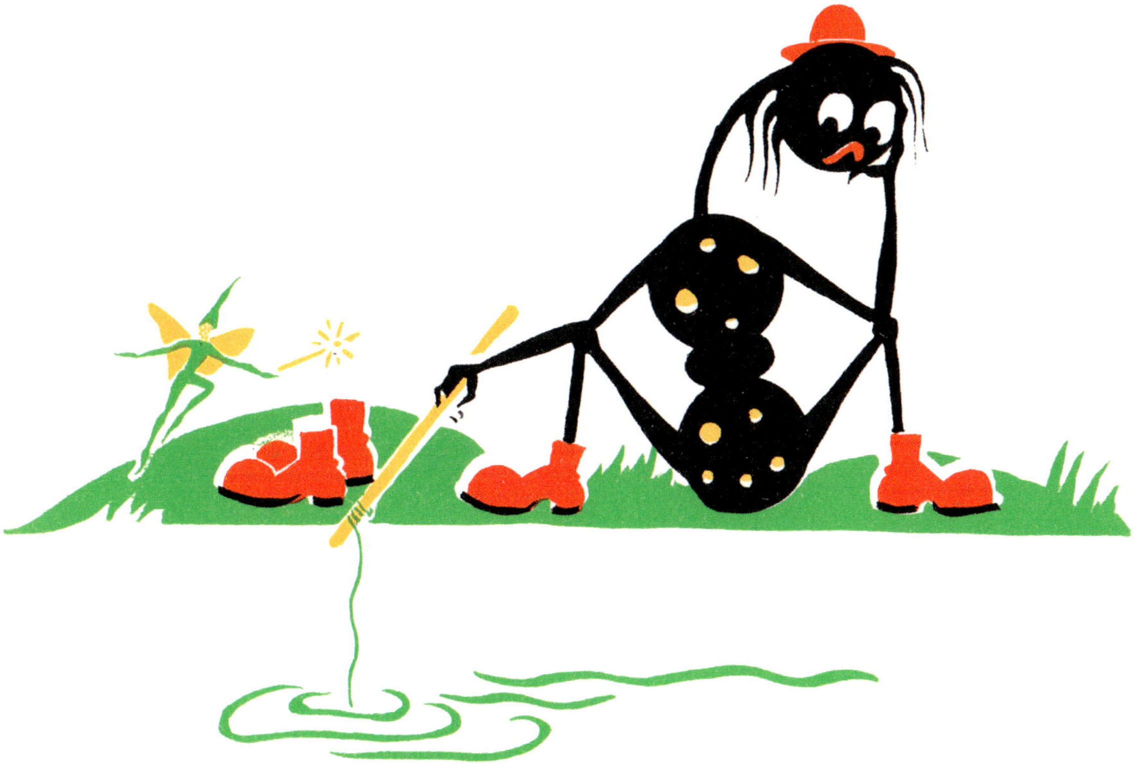

Up she flew, up, up and up… until she reached a silvery cloud, and from out of the snowy white fluff she dropped a pretty green bag.

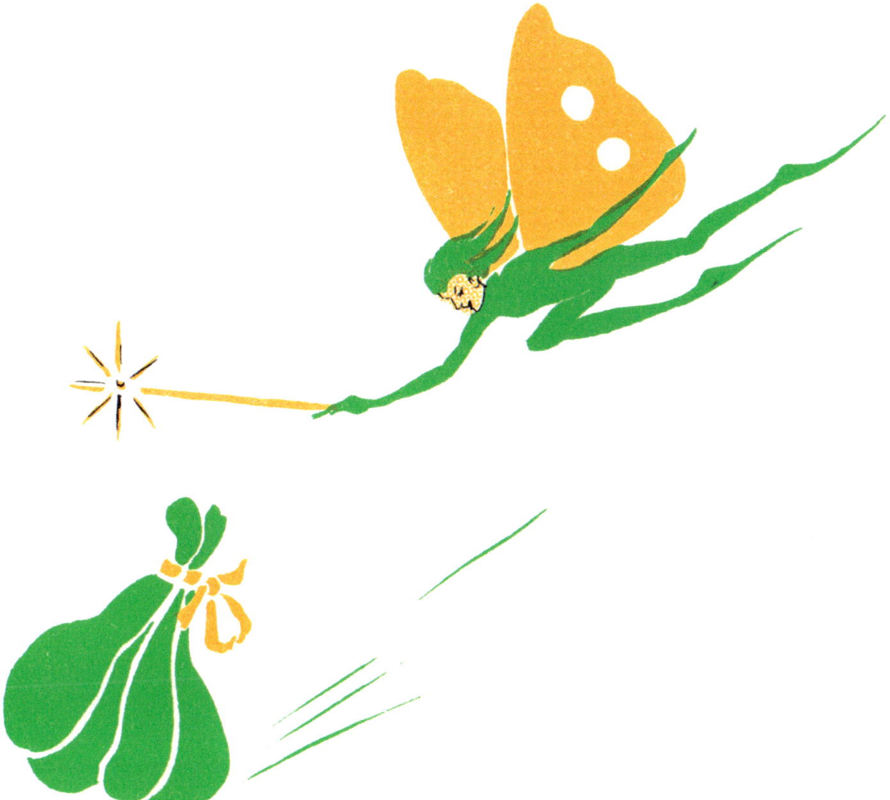

Down and down it fell! It landed right at the feet of Plonk. Out popped a little black head…

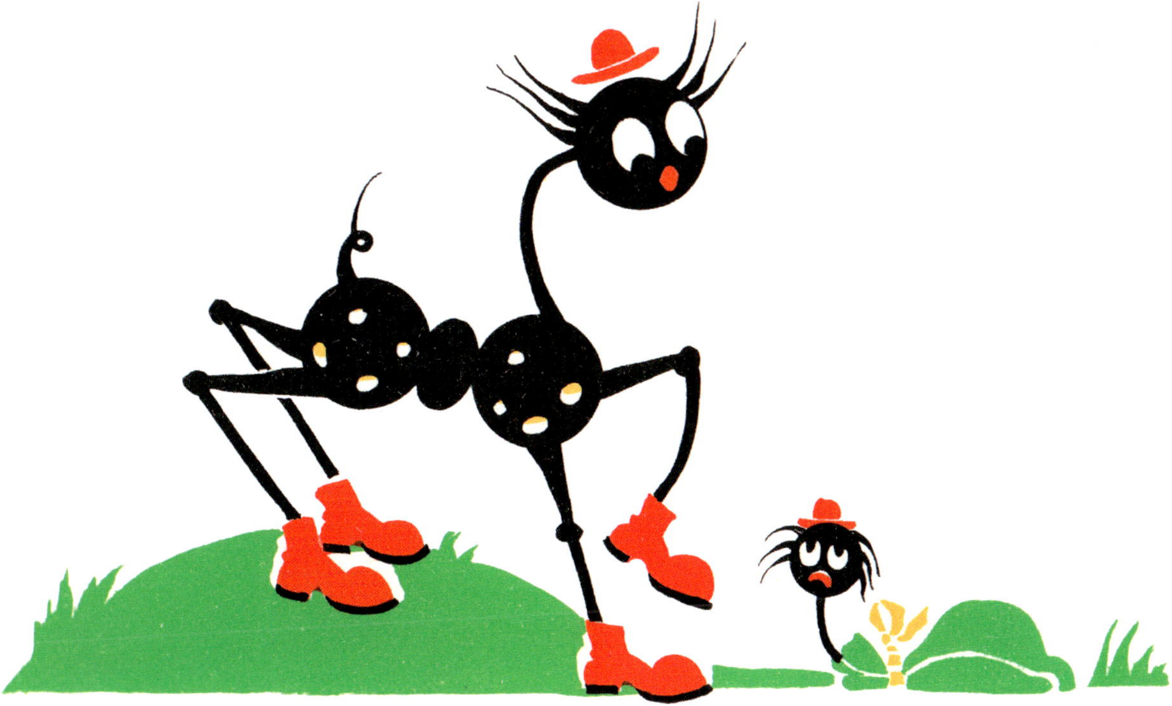

It was a little baby Plonk!

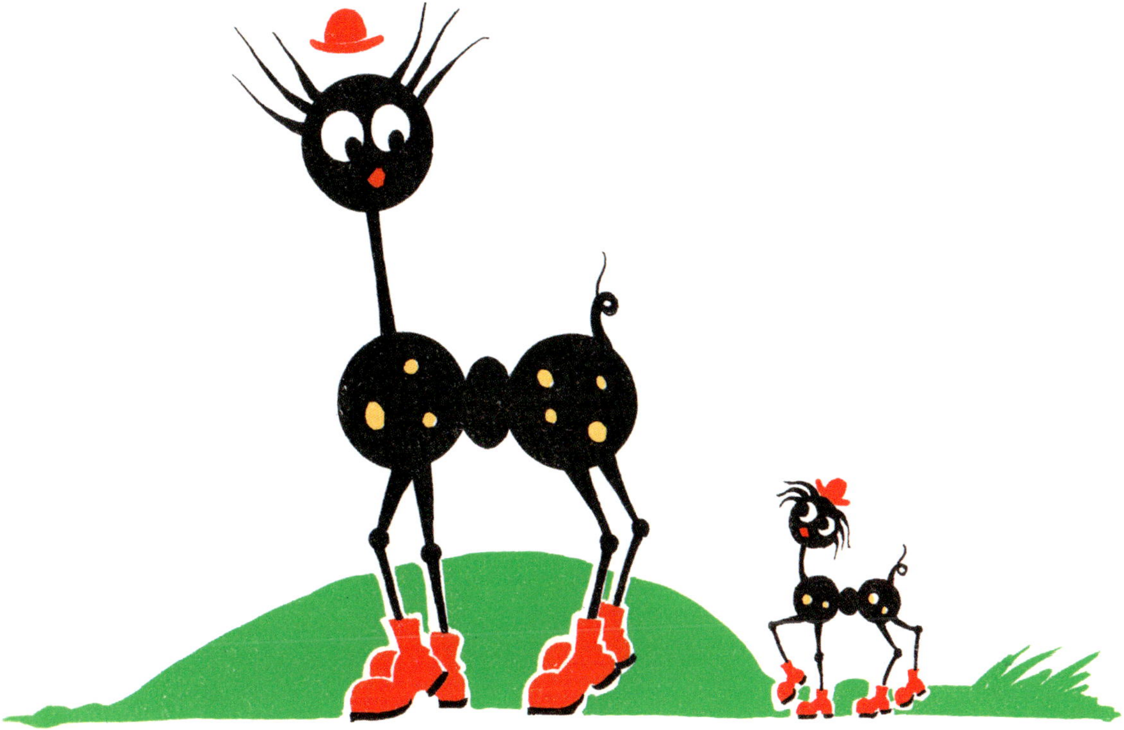

At first they were a little timid, and looked at one another curiously, but they soon became good friends…

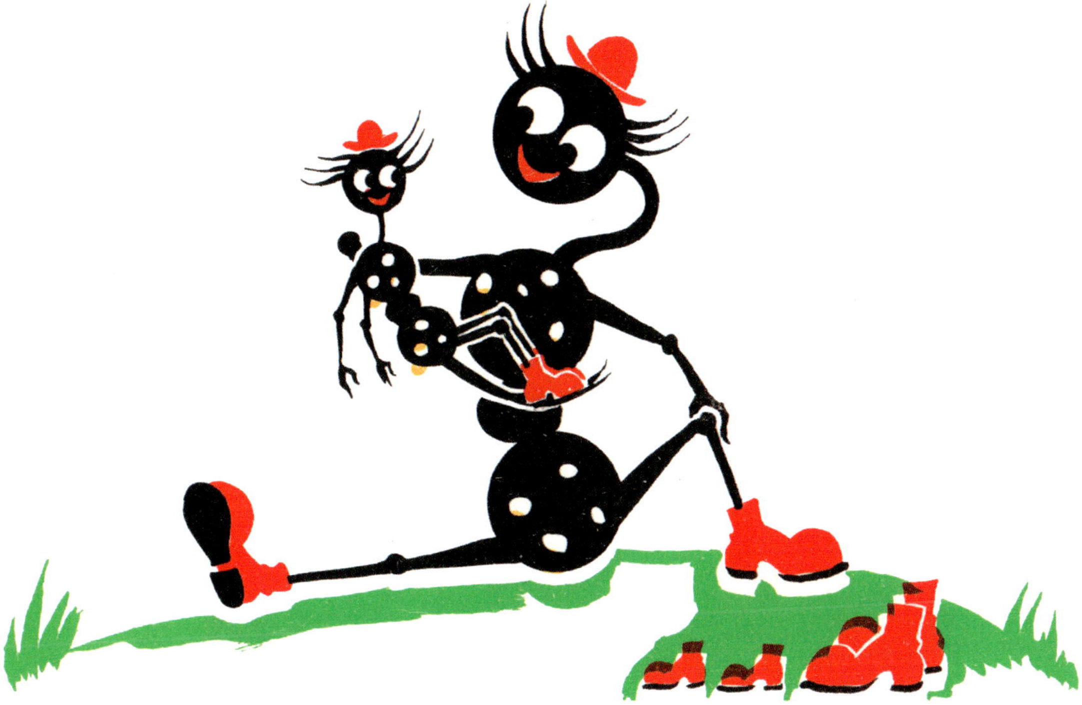

and Plonk decided to call the baby "Twinkle" because he seemed to have fallen from the stars…

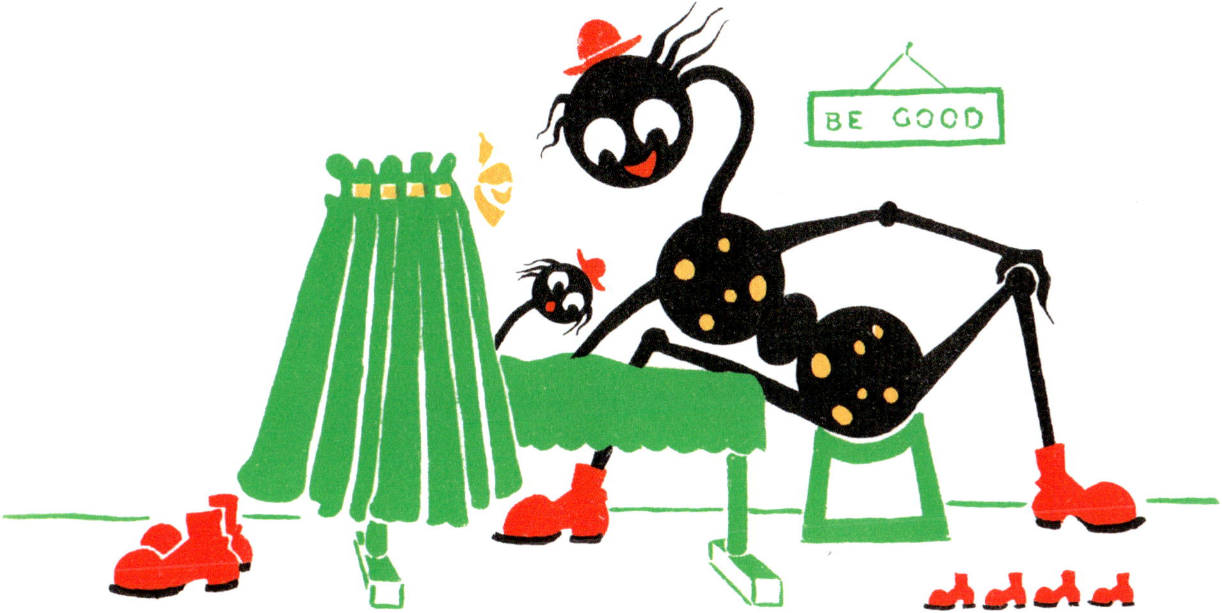
BE GOOD

and so Plonk and baby Twinkle lived happily ever afterwards.

⚜

Neither the witch, nor the pony-man, nor the farmer found out what had happened to him, but I think the little gnome had a good idea.

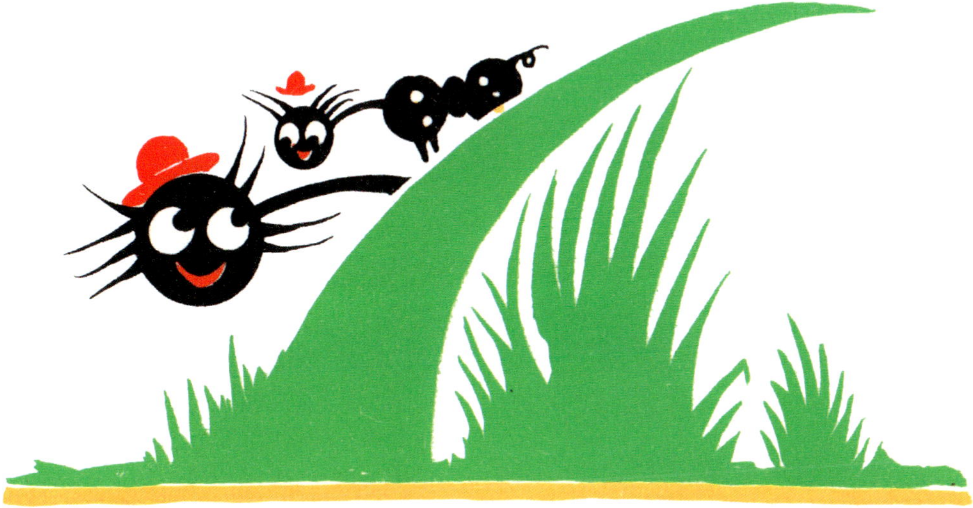

About the Author

At the age of 17 JOAN M. DAVIES won a scholarship to the Manchester School of Art for a 6 year training course (one of six places given throughout Great Britain) where she gained Distinction for both Anatomy and History of Architecture and studied under Mr Dodd, a tutor who studied under Picasso.

One of her oil paintings entitled *Romiley Bridge* was reviewed by L.S.Lowry in the Guardian, who said, "This is one of the coming artists of the day".

She started drawing Plonk from the shape of a farthing and the book was originally published in 1944.

In 2015 the much acclaimed fashion designer Hussein Chalayan MBE asked for permission to use some of the illustrations of Plonk for his show in Paris. His Spring/Summer collection 2016 entitled Pasatiempo (Cuba Calling) "Plonk clothes" which appeared on the catwalk are now being sold all over the world.

The author died in 1991 at the age of 69 years.